The Magic Vase

Fiona French

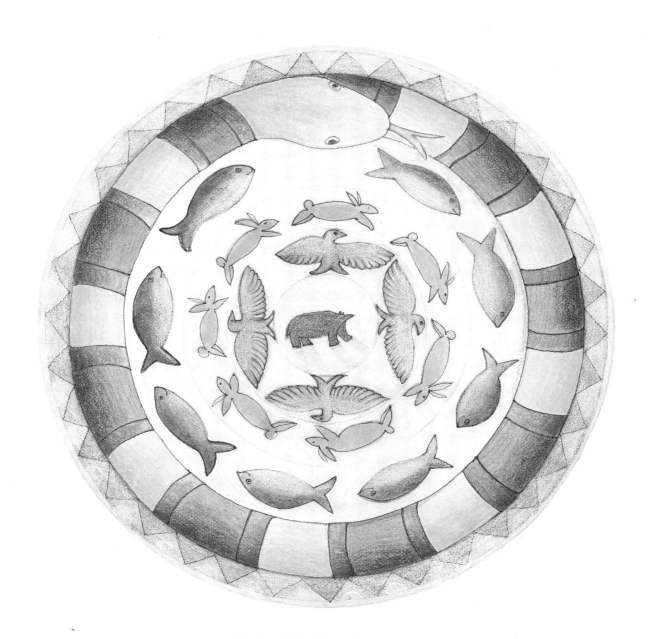

Oxford University Press

Once upon a time a rich art-dealer lived in a penthouse in the centre of a big city.

He bought and sold antique pots and vases, but he always kept the best ones for himself, until his collection was the second best in the world.

One day he heard that a very valuable vase had been found in the desert, and the dealer knew that if he could have this vase, his collection would then be the best in all the world.

So he got into his car and drove hundreds of miles until he reached a small dusty village. It was where he had been born.

'Where is this vase?' the art-dealer asked Maria the Potter.
He didn't waste time being polite.

Maria saw that the art-dealer had become a very greedy man.
'Perhaps I can show you this vase,' she said. 'I will bring it
to your motel tomorrow.'

That evening she made a magic vase.

She called to the snake in the desert,

'Come and help me show this man the value
of all things.'

The snake came out of the sand and wound his
coils around to make a vase shape. Maria
covered his coils with white clay.

She called to the bear on the mountain,

'Help me show this man the value of all things.'

Instantly the bear was a shape on the vase.
She called to the birds, to the rabbit, and to
the fishes, and they came to help too.

All her powers of magic made the vase look so
beautiful that the art-dealer was completely
tricked.

He wanted the vase very much but he was
cunning.

'This is not the vase I was looking for, but I
will give you a few dollars for it.'

'What a precious thing for my collection,' said the dealer, as he held the vase in his hands.

Just then it began to change. It grew brighter and became even richer.

'This vase is more beautiful than your storage jar from ancient Egypt,' whispered the fishes.

'And it is more valuable than your porcelain bowl from China,' whispered the rabbit.

'It is richer then the golden samovar from Russia,' cried the birds.

'And rarer than the bronze cauldron from Samarkand,' growled the bear.

The snake hissed,

'So, you will keep it in your penthouse and have the best collection in the world.'

'Yes, yes,' said the dealer. 'I will have the best collection in all the world.'

'See,' hissed the snake, 'this vase is not worth
a single cent.'

The snake uncoiled itself.

'Your collection of vases only belongs to you
during your lifetime.'

'And when you are dead,' said the snake, changing back to his real colours, 'they will be auctioned away and belong to someone else, and after that to someone else, and someone else.'

The snake dropped to

the ground and

wriggled

away

into

the

rocky

canyons.

'I've been tricked,' cried the art-dealer.

All the greed and anger poured out of his heart like liquid fire, and the memories of the hours in his life he had spent buying and selling the vases blew away like smoke into the desert.

The art-dealer went back to Maria.

'You have taught me the value of all things,' he said sadly. 'Now, I have nothing left.'

'But you still have your
wonderful collection,'
she answered, 'and here
is a small pot, as a gift, to
add to it.'

The art-dealer went back to his penthouse in the city a much wiser man. He looked at the vases and pots in a different way. He sold some and kept some and didn't even mind if one or two broke.

To the art-dealer himself, Maria's small gift from the village where he was born had made his collection the best in all the world.

For Lucy, Claire, and Libby,
and also for Phyllis

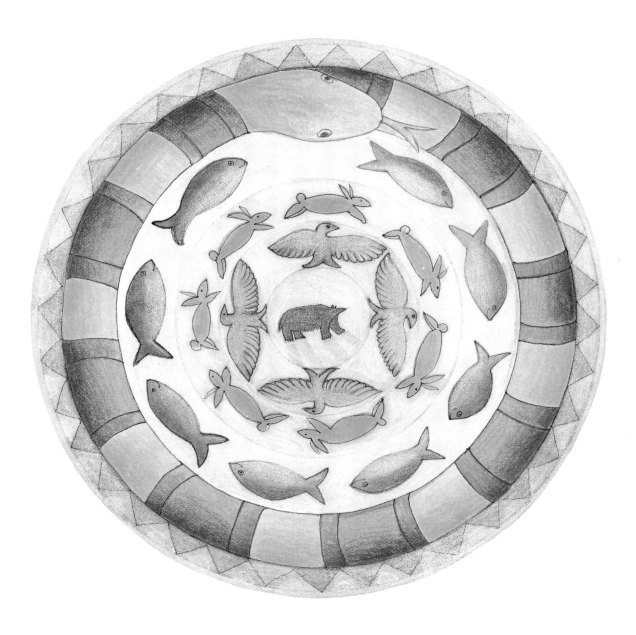

Oxford University Press, Walton Street, Oxford OX2 6DP

Oxford New York Toronto
Delhi Bombay Calcutta Madras Karachi
Petaling Jaya Singapore Hong Kong Tokyo
Nairobi Dar es Salaam Cape Town
Melbourne Auckland

and associated companies in
Berlin Ibadan

Oxford is a trade mark of Oxford University Press

British Library Cataloguing in Publication Data
French, Fiona, 1944–
The magic vase.
I. Title
823'.914 [J]

ISBN 0–19–279875–8

Printed in Hong Kong